Secrets of the
CRYSTAL CAVERN

by

Maggie Cary

Illustrations by

Anne-Marie Byrd

2011 © Maggie Cary
All rights reserved.

ISBN: 1463782594
ISBN-13: 9781463782597

They watched them by night,

And built them by day,

In hopes that the fairies

Would soon come to stay.

CHAPTER ONE

It started with a story. Twisted and magical it swept through our door on the summer night's breeze. My older cousin Dee and I sat on my bed in our grandparents' lake house, catching up on everything that had happened during the school year. It was the first Friday night since school had let out, and there was a lot to talk about.

Dee filled me in on her older sister Molly's string of boyfriends (cute versus not so cute), and I told her about my brother Jack's experiments and inventions (cool versus gross). We compared and complained about fifth grade and seventh grade, and how weird our parents were. We'd covered just about everything by the time my mom came upstairs with Jack close behind.

"Dee, your parents are looking for you downstairs. The Munchkin refuses to go to bed unless you pick out her PJs."

The Munchkin was Dee's younger sister, Melanie. Mom is the sort of person who comes up with what she considers cute nicknames for just about everyone under the age of thirty. Dee's full name is Danielle Marie, but when Mom started calling her Deedles, Dee managed to make it cool by shortening it.

I got stuck with String Bean. There's no cool way to shorten String Bean.

Dee gave me a quick hug, a quicker "g'night, Nina," and bounded down the stairs, her white-blond hair already working its way out of the braid that I'd spent the past thirty minutes styling.

I asked Mom if she would tell us a story, as she often did. I didn't know then that the story she was about to tell would affect our lives forever. Mom just sat on the end of my bed as usual, and Jack climbed up between us, leaning back against the wall under the eave. Mom said the story was about her and Aunt Sara, and when they had spent their childhood summers at Nanny and Papa's lake house, just like we were doing now.

Through the open window we heard waves lap the shore, and Mom told us about the beautiful fairies that had lived on the lake long ago. They had lived in little houses and needed little things, the size of Mom's dollhouse and miniature furniture, but not man or machine made. All the fairies' little things came from nature. Mom told us how she and Aunt Sara had built houses for the fairies.

I tossed my long brown hair over my shoulders and picked at my split ends, pulling them apart as I listened.

The little houses had pinecone-shingled roofs, Mom said, and flagstone steps that led to tiny front doors. The well, made from a walnut shell, was filled with fresh lake water for the fairies to drink. Mom and her sister would slice open fallen acorns and leave the nutmeats for the fairies to feast on when they flew in from their adventures.

Sticks and stones secured by mud and moss connected the many levels of the houses.

There were milkweed beds with the finest, silkiest white threads running through downy mattresses; there were mushroom tables and mussel-shell bathtubs.

"But sometimes, String Bean," Mom whispered, "the fairies would not fly in; they would come by boat."

I hate it when she calls me String Bean. It reminds me that I'm too straight and tall.

Mom told us she knew how the fairies got to their houses because when she went down to the shore, really early in the morning, she'd find their fairy boats. They would be sitting there empty, just beyond the reach of the waves. Small, slipper-shaped, open shells with a bench carved across the middle for the fairies to sit on had appeared from nowhere. If Mom didn't pick them up, they would disappear at dusk, just as mysteriously as they had arrived. Mom knew it meant the fairies had come during the night.

My brother, Jack, eight-year-old creative genius, made up a poem about Mom and her fairy houses. He recited it:

> *"They watched them by night*
> *And built them by day,*
> *In hopes that the fairies*
> *Would soon come to stay".*

He twisted his baseball cap round his head from back to front, his dark-green eyes large and round as saucers. He looks like my mom with ears that fit right, unlike mine, which don't. All the girls in his class like him, but Jack doesn't realize it, even when they make a big deal about every little genius thing he does.

We were so taken with Mom's story that first weekend that Dee, Jack, and I decided to build fairy houses too. Dee was thirteen, two years older than I am, and she thought constructing little houses using natural materials would be fun.

I had a magical feeling as we built a stick house and filled it with furniture made from rocks, twigs, and nuts. We carpeted the floor with fresh green moss. I felt as if the fairies would know we cared, and would come visit us. Jack was upset that we couldn't supply the tiny house with a tiny DVD player and microwave, but we reminded him that the fairies didn't need Blu-ray; they needed peace and quiet to spin their magic.

"And who ever heard of a fairy using a microwave?" I asked. "Next thing you'll want is to arrange pizza delivery for them."

"You're so lame," replied Jack.

Sometimes he just doesn't get me. He thinks I'm being serious when I'm actually making fun of him. I'm just three years older, but some days he really acts like a baby brother.

As we were teasing Jack, Dee's sister Molly walked by us on her way to meet friends who were waiting in the boat at the dock.

"Don't tell me you've been listening to those crazy stories your mother tells you. Get real!" She laughed at us as she jumped into the boat. We ignored her teenage snarkiness and spent the day adding finishing touches to the decorated houses.

The weekend ended too soon, as usual, and Dee and her family headed back to Boston. It was also time for Mom and Dad to go back to the city. Jack and I got to stay behind at the lake.

"Mom, I wish you didn't have to leave," I said as Jack and I walked them to the car. Even though I liked staying with my grandparents, I still had a funny feeling in my stomach and a lump in my throat when my parents left on Sunday night.

"You'll have a great week, Nina, and it's much nicer here than in the city," Dad said. "Nanny and Papa will keep you company. And you also have Scout."

Hearing her name, Scout danced around us and barked twice, as if confirming Dad's words.

"I'll see you in just five days," Mom promised. "Maybe if you keep your eyes open, you'll see a fairy." She winked at us. Then she gave us both a long hug and a kiss and got into the car. Jack looked like he was ready to cry as we waved goodbye.

CHAPTER TWO

Papa laughed when Jack asked him about the fairies. "Pixies," he chuckled. "Pixies in the woods. Sounds like your mother and her half-baked stories. When she was about your age, she played for hours out at those little houses she made. Pixies! You've got your mother's imagination, Jack." He was still laughing as he headed outside with his gardening tools.

"I miss Mom and Dad," said Jack.

"Oh, don't mind your grandfather, Jack," Nanny consoled. She had on her floppy, large-brimmed gardening hat and was walking more slowly than Papa, carrying her gardening gloves and pruners so she could tend to her roses.

"Your parents will be back here before you know it," Nanny reassured Jack. I was sure she was right. After the first day without Mom and Dad, Jack would be fine and so busy that he wouldn't have time to miss them.

We worked on the fairy houses a little, but it wasn't the same without Dee. She's a nature expert. Science is her thing and she knows how to make the most out of what we find in the woods.

"When Dee comes on the weekend, we'll gather milkweed on the other side of the Point. Okay, Jack?" I said.

"Okay, but I don't get why we have to be stuck here."

When he's moody like that, Jack likes to do something "relaxing." Sometimes it might be digging for worms; other times it might be building a replica of the Empire

State Building with his Erector Set. This time, he decided to fish. He stood on the end of the dock, casting his fishing line into the lake and reeling in one sunfish after another.

"Wow! Jack, that's quite a catch," said Papa, walking to the end of the dock. He smiled and shook his head as he looked into the rusty bait bucket where Jack was saving the fish he'd caught. "Looks like you've caught tonight's dinner!"

I knew Nanny had probably told Papa to check on Jack and not to tease him anymore about the fairies. Seeing my chance as Jack was talking to Papa, I said, "Jack, can you help me?"

"Not now, Nina, I'm working on a record."

"Please, Jack," I pleaded. "Oh, hi, Papa." I turned back to Jack. "I need your help with the dollhouses," I whispered.

"See you later, kids," Papa said, smiling. He returned to the house.

"Okay, Nina," Jack sighed. He reeled in his line and walked over to the bucket. "See you guys tomorrow when I catch you again," he said as he poured the bucket of fish back to freedom. He leaned his fishing pole against the side of the shed and looked at me. "So. What's up?"

"I'm rearranging some of the dollhouses, and I need your help lifting them. I was thinking we could surprise Mom by dusting them off and cleaning out the spider webs." I was really excited about my new project, and thought it would be even more fun if I had company.

"I traded fishing for cleaning dollhouses?" he moaned. "Oh, all right." I felt kind of bad that he'd thrown away his chance to break his fishing record. But he came along anyway.

My mom's dollhouses are very realistic, complete with furniture, rugs, wallpaper, pictures, and props. Mini checker sets and vases all needed to be dusted. I wiped down each doll with a tissue and put it in a freshly cleaned spot. The minister of the white-steepled church welcomed a little family. In the general store, the storekeeper sold miniature candy canes to a tiny boy from the log cabin. The mother in the log cabin stood next to the apples and piecrust in the kitchen.

My favorite dolls were in the Victorian mansion. They had porcelain faces, hands, and feet, and fancy flowered dresses with bustles at the back. Mom and I had found them on a rainy Saturday in an antique store in North Conway. I'd named them Jobeth and Milly. You could tell by looking at them that they were sisters. I made Jobeth the serious, stern one, and Milly the one who was always doing something funny and outrageous, by Victorian standards, anyway.

We spent the rest of that afternoon cleaning out and setting up the dollhouses. Although he'd kill me if I ever told his friends, Jack really enjoyed himself. Tired from our busy day of cleaning, we had no problem falling asleep that night. If we'd known what was ahead of us, things would have been different.

CHAPTER THREE

We woke early the next morning, and before we'd even had breakfast, Jack and I ran down to the old swing set Papa had put up thirty years ago. After only a couple of minutes, the air changed; we sensed a nasty storm approaching. We felt the temperature cool and the breeze from the east pick up.

The lake storm started quickly. White-capped waves rose almost instantaneously, higher and higher, lashing against the dock. Then the wind really started to blast, sending leaves, pine needles, twigs, and small branches scattering across the lawn. The larger trees began to bow in the wind.

Boats rocked wildly on their moorings, up and down, back and forth. An old dinghy at the dock broke free from one of its lines and crashed into the wooden post it was still tied to. I felt tingles from the electrical storm before I saw the lightning.

Around the Point I could see the rain racing across the lake. Without a word, Jack and I tore off running back to the house as the lightning crashed behind us.

"Just made it, did you?" Papa commented calmly from his easy chair by the fireplace. The clocks in the living room chimed all at once. Papa was a time freak and there were clocks everywhere, ticking and chiming all day in unison. Big clocks, naval clocks, calendar clocks—they covered the walls throughout the old house. Every morning without fail, Papa patiently wound each clock that needed it. Every hour, the massive grandfather clock in the front hall gonged the hour, and all the other clocks joined in, dinging, clanging, and cuckooing. Scout whimpered and scurried under the kitchen table.

Nanny turned on the portable radio in the kitchen. "Severe storm warnings expected through tonight," warned the deep voice on the radio. "Take immediate shelter! Those of you living in mobile..." Nanny turned off the radio.

"We've got to save the batteries. Sounds like a bad storm," Nanny said to no one in particular. The sky had gone black and the house was so dark inside that it looked like nighttime. Nanny reached into the hutch for candles and grabbed the long matches she kept on the fireplace. "It's good to be prepared, just in case," she said, talking to whomever she was talking to in the first place.

As Nanny placed the candles on the table, the electricity went out as if on cue. She lit them just a few seconds after the lights went off. The storm continued throughout the day. It was kind of scary in the house with the wind howling, the pounding rain, and the hail bouncing off the windows. But it was a heck of a lot better than being outside. We played board games and watched the storm as it twisted branches off the trees and whipped the lake until it looked like the ocean had that time we were vacationing on the Cape at Hyannis, when Hurricane Donna unexpectedly brushed the coast.

I was scared, but Nanny made us chocolate milk and Papa tended a crackling fire that made us feel cozy. We went to bed early, with the old moose head looking wearily down on me as the rain continued to pound on the windows and the roof. Despite the force of the storm, there was something soothing about the drone of the wind and the sound of the rain on the roof that lulled me to sleep in no time.

It seemed like I had just gone to sleep, but when I woke I knew it was the middle of the night. Everything was quiet. The rain and the wind had stopped, and the night sounds of the woods were hushed. No owls hooted, no loons called, and the crickets were silent. I felt my way out of bed and headed downstairs to the bathroom. I knew I should have gone before I went to bed.

I was walking through the kitchen on my way back from the bathroom when I noticed it was bright outside. Looking out the big picture window, I could see the moon was full over the lake and the stars were bright in the sky. But it seemed brighter than the moon and stars could possibly make it, even on their best nights.

I noticed a light that appeared to be coming right off the lake, not from the sky. Goosebumps ran down my spine. The translucent water glittered like crystals. It was the most beautiful light I had ever seen. Golden rays touching down on the lake beneath the full moon seemed to be dancing a silent ballet. I scrambled upstairs in the dark to wake Jack.

I found my brother still fast asleep and noticed, turning toward the window, that I couldn't see the light anymore. It was the middle of the night, I was tired, and despite the fading glow on the lake, I lay down and fell asleep before I realized I had closed my eyes.

CHAPTER FOUR

As if it had been no more than a dream, I didn't remember the crystal light at first when I woke up in the morning. I found Jack in front of the downstairs TV. The sun was shining when Nanny called us away from our cartoons for breakfast.

"It's much too nice a day to be couch potatoes," she said as she put down plates of blueberry pancakes smothered in melted butter and hot maple syrup. "I have to take Papa to town to see the eye doctor, so you're on your own today. There are cold cuts and blueberry cake in the fridge; don't forget to eat lunch."

"Jack, let's hike up Eagle Mountain and have a picnic lunch on top," I said, ready for an adventure after being cooped up the day before.

"Let's do it!" Jack raced out of the room to load his backpack. Scout was excited too, bouncing around, eager to go for a walk.

When Nanny and Papa left, we started on our way. I don't know who named the mountain behind our house "Eagle Mountain," because I've never seen any eagles up there. But it sure is high, and I suppose if there were eagles around here, they'd like it all right. We hiked up quietly, like the Native Americans would have done, careful not to step on twigs, looking for wildlife along the way.

"You can't see the animals if they hear you coming," Jack whispered. He carried a crooked stick that he swore was really a spear left by Native Americans. They must have camped nearby really recently, I thought, judging from the fine condition of the spear. Despite our stealth, we saw only a few birds on the way up, maybe because Scout, the wild wolf we Indians had trained to help us hunt, ran head of us, sniffing and digging at logs, holes, and trees.

After our long, circular trip to the mountaintop, we broke out our canteen and drank fresh stream water, which tasted a lot like Nanny's lemonade. As we lay on our backs on the rocks in a little clearing at the top of the hill, eating our cheese sandwiches and staring up at the few scattered clouds, time seemed to stand still. Finding pictures in the clouds, we told our favorite stories to each other, picked the blueberries out of the cake Nanny had sent with us, and passed the afternoon.

We could tell from the sun that it was getting late. Scout eagerly led the way back, long bored with us, except for when Jack dropped a piece of cake. By the time we got back to the house, Nanny and Papa had come back from the doctor, loaded down with two big bags of corn on the cob. As Papa and Scout disappeared into the kitchen, Nanny called to us, "Please take these out on the stoop and shuck them."

We quickly stripped the corn, leaving time for me to climb the rocks to Needle

Point before dinner. I sat on the cliff there, looking toward the lake that spilled out for miles in front of me. I had brought my journal to scribble a few notes. This was my thinking place, where my world stretched out before me and my daydreams came alive.

It's funny, but sitting there perched high above the lake, I often imagined the ghosts of dead Native Americans, their spirits running along the shoreline—fetching water and hunting deer, their children playing along the banks of the cove. I could feel the presence of their spirits. It left me feeling peaceful as I sat on my cliff looking at the place where the bay leads to town.

"Nina, Nina," I heard Nanny calling. She must have been calling for a while. I looked over to see her waving from the dock. She always knew where to find me. "Dinnertime! Come get washed up."

"Coming Nan," I called, waving back to her. I got up off my perch and headed toward the house, leaving the spirits behind on my cliff.

CHAPTER FIVE

It was Friday again, and Jack and I stayed close to the house listening for Mom and Dad's car. In the afternoon, we played Whiffle ball in the driveway with D.J., a boy from down the street. First base was a pine tree, second and third were the boys' shirts, and home plate was the welcome mat decorated with a black Labrador retriever with a duck in its mouth, which we borrowed from the front porch.

We took turns whacking the Wiffle ball, running wildly around the bases and kicking up the dust from the dirt driveway. I didn't even know we were keeping score, but Jack announced that it was 12 to 10 to 9—his lead, of course—just before D.J. was called home to dinner.

As dusk set in, we too were called inside for a dinner of hot dogs, chips, and molasses-sweetened baked beans, our favorite meal. Dee and her family had arrived, but immediately after unloading their stuff they went into town to have dinner at the Pizza Shack. After throwing out our paper plates and cups from dinner, Jack and I settled into playing cards at the dining room table.

Mom and Dad still hadn't arrived when Nanny, getting up from the TV, called to us, "Kids, get ready for bed." We slipped on our pajamas, washed our hands and faces, and brushed our teeth. We were in bed reading when I heard Nanny answer the phone downstairs. I could hear her voice through the cracks in the wall.

"Oh, that's a shame, but you really shouldn't drive if it's that bad. We'll have lunch for you when you get here tomorrow. They're in bed. Yes, I'll let them know. Good night, honey."

A few moments later I heard Nanny padding slowly up the stairs. "That was your mom on the phone. She says the weather is awful and there are severe storm warnings in northern Massachusetts tonight. They don't want to risk driving through it at night, so they'll leave in the morning and be here tomorrow by lunch. She sends a big kiss for each of you. She says she's sorry and they can't wait to see you."

When Nanny left, I tried to think of something to say that would make Jack feel better. Although he slept in the corner of the adjoining room, I could still hear the crack in his voice as he tried to muffle his tears.

"They promised, Nina," he said.

"I know," I said, "but you know they'd come if they could." We lay there quietly for a long time.

I woke when the rain began to tap lightly on the roof and then to pound down. I got up to close the windows. The curtains blew wildly as I cranked the handle toward me. White-capped waves on the lake were crashing over our anchored raft, looking like they might pull the chained float from its moorings.

The trees bowed over like in the last storm, and the leaves flew from the birch trees in the front yard. Just as I gave the stiff window crank one last turn in order to keep the wind and rain outside, I noticed a small flickering light—that crystal light again, squished against the window pane. A tiny, pale, moonlit, human-like face looked up at me. Rubbing my eyes, I peered down at the unbelievable sight, trying to get a better look. I spoke out loud, not believing my own words: "It's a... it's a... a... fairy!"

In the strobe lighting provided by the lightning shooting through the night sky, I saw that the beautiful creature was trapped between the window and the screen, beating its wet wings against the glass. I opened the window back up and carefully took down the screen.

Jack, who must have been awakened by the last loud thunder boom, entered my room.

"Nina, close the window." Annoyed, he asked, "What do you think you're doing?"

"Help me, Jack! It's a fairy trapped in the window! Take the screen," I heard myself say, too amazed to believe this was real.

Jack saw it too. "What the heck! I must be dreaming," he mumbled, shaking his head.

The visitor jumped off the screen and flew like a wounded bird into our room. Unlike any bird I had ever seen, though, tiny beams of light projected from it. Jack snapped awake at this strange sight and ran over to turn on the small light next to my bed.

As the fairy flew into the pale lamplight like a scared moth, Nanny's cat, Cheetah, who liked to sleep in my room, lunged at the creature as if it were a tasty bug to eat.

Jack, with the quickness of an all-star Wiffle ball shortstop, grabbed Cheetah in midair and tossed her toward the door in one smooth motion. He opened the door and chased her out as she meowed angrily at this sudden interruption of her sleep and then her hunt.

We watched in amazement as the tiny fairy treaded air like a hummingbird over the lamp, its feet moving constantly beneath

its wings. I reached out with my
ing to cup it without damaging
wings. I could see that the wings glistened,
like sparkling toothpaste or maybe shimmery paint. But the wings had lots of colors
mixed in, not just one.

Glittery dust fell onto my fingers as the
fairy lay in the palm of my hand. It was the
size of a large moth, with a head and face
shaped like a person's. It had short, dark
hair, emerald eyes, and a tiny red mouth.

We stared at the fairy, and it stared warily
back at us.

"I think it's hurt, Jack," I said. "Look how
its body trembles."

"I know," Jack said. "Let's put it in one
of our fairy houses." He spoke calmly to the
fairy. "We've made you a nice home and a
cozy bed." He looked at me. "But I'll bet the
storm has blown it to pieces."

"I know," I announced, "you can sleep here. I've got just the place." I carried the weary fairy to my favorite dollhouse, the Victorian mansion.

"I've got a beautiful four-poster canopy bed for you," I said, carefully tucking the fairy beneath the ruffled pink covers of the dollhouse bed and pulling the bedspread around the tiny, frail creature. It closed its eyes immediately and fell into a deep sleep. Still feeling as if I might be dreaming, I turned to my brother.

"Jack, this is real, isn't it? I mean, there really is a fairy in our room, isn't there?"

"Yep," he said, as if this were a normal occurrence. "We should get some sleep, though, so we can get up early to ask the fairy all about itself."

He went back to bed and soon I heard him softly snoring. I was way too excited to sleep.

I lay in my bed, watching the Victorian house for what seemed like hours. At some point, though, my overwhelmed brain turned off, and I fell into a deep but brief sleep.

CHAPTER SIX

The bright morning sunshine streamed into my room from the east. I jumped out of my bed when I saw Jack hunched over the dollhouse, and ran over to see if the fairy was still there.

The fairy, sitting up in the canopy bed, opened its mouth in a silent scream. A giant monster eye was looking down at the frightened creature, who fell back onto the lace pillow, nearly fainting from the sight of the terrible beast.

Jack leaned the magnifying glass back, like he was a detective in a movie, and saw the tiny creature sit up, shaking, and then fall back against the pillow.

"JACK! What are you doing? You should be watching it, not scaring it!" I pushed him aside. Then I remembered to lower my voice. "It wasn't a dream, it's really still here," I murmured. "I can't believe it! Mom knew all along that they're real, she wasn't just telling us stories!"

"I know," said Jack. "But how do you know if it's a boy or a girl?"

"Why, it's a girl of course, you silly, look at her face." The fairy seemed to sneer up at us. "Oh, my mistake," I quickly apologized, "it's a boy." The fairy grinned and then passed out again.

"Well, what are we going to do with him?" Jack asked, as we leaned against the dollhouse, watching the fairy sleep.

"Mom would know what to do, but with her new job, I don't think we should bother her. We can handle this on our own," I said.

"Besides, she always told us that if you want to see fairy magic, you must keep it to yourself, in your heart. It's a secret magical thing, not something you talk about."

"I think he's waking up again!" Jack exclaimed. The tiny fairy slowly opened his eyes and looked up at us, and I imagined what it would be like to see the giant faces of two human children. The fairy opened his mouth as if to speak, but we didn't hear anything.

Suddenly the fairy pulled down the bed covers and shot up from the sheets, flying up to Jack's right ear and batting his wings together. Fairy dust fluttered down onto Jack's ear and I heard the rapid beating of wings. The fairy flew over to his other ear and sprinkled more silver dust from his painted wings. Then he flew over to my ears and did the same thing.

Jack tilted his head. I heard it too—a squirrel running up a tree outside the window. I think he realized at the same moment I did that we were suddenly hearing all sorts of sounds coming from outside, sounds we had never heard before. It seemed like I could even hear the ants marching up the side of the house, looking for new shelter after the recent storms. I supposed that the fairy dust was allowing us to hear every little sound from the woods across the street.

"Whoa!" Jack and I said together, delighted at our fantastic hearing. But then the fairy collapsed back into the bed as quickly as he had sprung out of it.

"Where am I?" he asked weakly, but very clearly.

"You're in the Victorian mansion in our bedroom," I said, still not used to the idea of talking to a fairy.

"How did I get here?"

"The storm blew you in on a gust of wind and we rescued you from Nanny's cat. If it wasn't for us, you'd be catnip," bragged Jack. This was not, of course, entirely true, as Cheetah really never got that close to catching the fairy, but I wasn't about to explain Jack's tendency to exaggerate.

"Shall we keep you and you can live here with Jobeth and Milly?" I asked. The surprised fairy looked over at the two stiff Victorian dolls, shuddered, and fainted back into the fancy sheets again.

Annoyed by the fairy's apparent lack of courage, Jack asked, "Are you *sure* it's not a girl?"

CHAPTER SEVEN

I entered my room to find Jack sitting with his back to the fairy, wrapped up in a noisy handheld video game in which he was a soldier. I ran over to the dollhouse and peered into the bedroom window. Seeing the frightened look on the fairy's face, I yelled, "Jack! I told you to watch him! Turn that off!"

The fairy must have been terrified by the exploding, screeching, and pounding noises filling the room. Noises like the bulldozers made when they toppled trees and destroyed his forest.

I spoke softly and calmly to the fairy, hoping to settle him down. "Here. I've brought you fresh milkweed to sleep in. Mom always said that's what fairies like best." I removed the dolls that seemed to have bothered him. "Don't worry. You don't have to stay with Jobeth and Milly if you don't want to."

As the fairy appeared to calm down a little, I continued. "I had to walk halfway around the Point to get this. I hope it's okay." I split the milkweed down the middle, opening it up and spreading out the silky fluff inside it on the dollhouse floor. Then I gently helped him into the new bed.

A white liquid oozed from the end of the milkweed pod, and the tiny creature turned his face into it and drank, slurping furiously. I hadn't realized how hungry he was. I had forgotten how Mom had explained that the milkweed not only made good fairy beds, but that the fairies got milk from it as well.

"Look, Jack! He's drinking the milk."

We watched, engrossed, as the fairy drank and then lay back on the silky threads of the milkweed. He looked much more comfortable there than he had in the canopy bed.

We continued to gaze at him as he fell asleep again. I supposed that the awful storms, the cat, Jobeth and Milly, and two curious children had taken a lot out of him. An hour passed as we watched him lie motionless. After a time, we realized that he was awake and crying silently. Moist droplets rolled down his pale cheeks.

"My family," the fairy sobbed. "I lost my family in the storm. I was out in the woods gathering nectar when the storm grew fierce. I was supposed to be home by dinner. My sister, Lily, where can she be? I must find her!" He fell back into the milkweed husk.

"Oh! He has a family," I said."I hope they're all right. We'll find them."

"Yeah. Don't worry, just rest," said Jack. "We'll find your family."

The weak fairy voice, sounding a little less frantic, said, "You will? You are so kind. But if you are to find my Lily, remember, beware of the bandits. They eat fish and fairy for dinner!"

"Huh? Who are the bandits?" asked Jack.

"Why, they are those nasty creatures with the black rings beneath their eyes, like masks, and stripes on their tails. Please find my sister!" he pleaded.

We ran down the stairs and headed out on our search. Where we were going to look, we didn't know. Nanny told us to be careful if we were going out after the storm. It was dangerous. There could be electrical wires and tree limbs waiting to fall on us.

As we left, we saw the big birch tree with the birdhouse in it lying across the front lawn. It had just missed the house. Papa stood on the grass surveying the damage.

"Morning, Papa," we called as we ran down the front path toward the lake.

"Careful now. Storm's turned everything upside down," he called back.

"Where do we look first?" Jack asked. "Won't finding a fairy be like finding a needle in a haystack?"

"We'll just have to look," I answered, knowing he was right but not wanting to discourage him. We searched the lakeshore around the house most of the morning, while taking turns sneaking back and checking on our fairy. We decided that even if we could have used the help, it wasn't a good idea to tell anyone about him. Each time I looked in on him, I noted that the fairy lay in a restless sleep. By the time Nanny called us in for lunch, we were tired and frustrated.

CHAPTER EIGHT

After lunch we checked on the fairy once again, and then went back outside to look for his sister. All afternoon we looked everywhere we could think of—along the shore, deep into the woods, and up and down the roadway. Jack repeatedly complained that it was "like finding a needle in a haystack."

I was about ready to agree and give up when I saw Jack staring up from under the eaves below the short, flat overhang on the side of the house. He was watching a large spider scrambling on a web.

"Wonder why he's in such a hurry?" he thought aloud, as the spider moved toward the center of its web. "Nina! Over here!" he yelled, not seeing that I was right next to him.

"I see it!" I yelled back.

Underneath the gutter was an enormous web, and a huge spider hurrying toward a beautiful butterfly caught in the glistening threads.

"It must be the other fairy!" I shrieked, but Jack had already seen it. Turning over a trash can, he leaped up and snatched the fairy just as the spider moved in to make its kill. Jack carefully pulled the web strands from her, breaking them into sticky pieces that looked like cotton candy.

"You found her! All right!" I cheered. As he lifted the fairy, she looked at the terrible jaws of the angry spider, and then back at Jack.

"You saved me!" she cried, and she flew from his hands up to our ears and sprinkled us with fairy dust. He smiled.

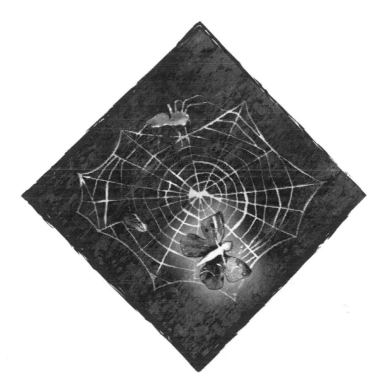

CHAPTER NINE

Lily told us that the storm had risen from the lake quickly, before the fairies had had time to find shelter. She had been battered and then swept away by the torrential rain. She'd lost sight of her brother after he was ripped away from her by the wind. She said time had seemed to slow, amplifying each life-threatening moment as she blew through space, helpless. But then a gust of wind had flipped her into a protected area by the side of a house.

When she had finally stopped falling, she said, she seemed to have landed on a springy, sticky net, one that caught her and held her tightly in midair. Her feelings of relief from escaping the wind's fury lasted only seconds before her self-preservation instinct reasserted itself.

She had been dizzy and confused and tried to sit up but could not. She'd looked around and realized, in absolute horror, that she had been tossed into a spider's web!

Lily described how she had struggled. But the more she fought, the tighter the web became around her, trapping her wings and leaving her unable to fly. She told us she'd known she shouldn't struggle; she'd been taught to avoid spider webs at all costs, but knew that if she was caught in one, the best thing to do was nothing. But she had panicked in the fear of the moment.

Lily said she'd stilled herself and hoped her brother, Luna, would find her when the wind calmed. He was sure to find her, she'd believed, but if not, she knew that the stickiness would dry up in about a day, allowing her to wriggle away and escape, if only she could remain still. If she moved, she knew the spider would sense her, and move in to eat her alive.

Lily recalled that her arms and legs had begun to grow numb as she nearly fell asleep. She was beaten and exhausted from the storm, but she knew she needed to remain alert if she wanted to live. She told us she'd been shivering, and then she'd sneezed. She hadn't felt it coming. She had been trapped in the web for hours. She was wet and cold, but she was still more afraid than uncomfortable.

Jack and I shivered too, just hearing about Lily's close call. The spider must have felt the twitching of the net and decided it was dinnertime. Lily said she'd lost hope as the spider swiftly slid down its web to check on the day's catch. She had been sure it was too late until Jack had suddenly grabbed her, saving her life.

CHAPTER TEN

"My, I'm sticky," the fairy said, fluttering in Jack's hands as we rushed past our grandparents in the kitchen and up to our room.

"Shhh," we hushed her, afraid someone would hear, even though I was sure that Nanny's and Papa's ears had not been sprinkled with fairy dust.

"Where's the fire?" called Papa after us.

We burst into my bedroom, excited to show Luna we'd found his sister. I slammed the door and locked it behind us.

"Look, we found her!" cried Jack. We bent over the dollhouse, and Lily flew down into her brother's little room.

"Ohhh, Luna!" she cried. "Look at you." She flittered around her brother, inspecting him closely, concern spreading across her tiny features.

Bumping our heads as we bent over to get a better look, we saw that Luna did not look well at all. He smiled at his sister but could barely lift his head off the pillow to greet her.

"You are safe…thank goodness," he said, smiling briefly again before drifting off to sleep.

"My brother is not well," Lily said, finally looking up at me with teary eyes. "I must stay here with him."

In order to avoid suspicion or Nanny coming into the room without warning, Jack went down to help with dinner. We agreed he would keep an eye on Nanny and Papa to make sure they didn't surprise me and the fairies. I stayed and watched Lily while she watched her brother.

After sitting silently for what seemed like hours, but could only have been minutes, Lily spoke. "He is weak. We must watch him carefully."

"I didn't realize he was so sick," I said. "I thought he was just tired."

"See how his face is flushed?" Lily looked directly at me. "Healthy fairy faces are pale; he has too much color."

After dinner we told Nanny we were tired from our long day and were going to bed early. She wanted to take our temperatures, and she felt Jack's forehead. Papa said he wanted to call the local newspaper to report this unusual occurrence.

"We're just tired, Nan," I replied, eager to check on our guests. And it was also the truth: we *were* exhausted from our adventures.

After looking in on the fairies and finding them both asleep, Lily at the foot of her brother's bed, I flopped down onto my own mattress.

We'd been so busy all day long, we had forgotten that Mom and Dad hadn't arrived. At dinner, Nanny told us that Mom had called earlier and informed her that travel was still too dangerous. The storm had been called the "storm of the century" by more than one weather station. Between Massachusetts and New Hampshire, there were flooded roads, downed power lines, and trees in the streets. The highway bridge over the Merrimack River had collapsed from the flooding. Mom had had to use her cell phone to call Nanny because the telephone lines at home were down.

As I lay there utterly exhausted, wanting to close my eyes and doze off but still too excited to sleep, thoughts of the day came

crashing into my head. I wished Mom we
here. Maybe I'd ask Nan if I could try to
call home tonight. I thought about what
Lily had said about Luna being sick. I had so
many questions jumbled up inside my head.
Could Mom have met fairies too when she
was here as a girl?

Jack came into the room and looked at the
visitors in the dollhouse. Reading his mind, I
said, "It's nothing we can talk about with anyone, Jack. Don't you feel that if we do, we'll
lose all the magic? People would think we are
just making up a story. 'What vivid imagina-
tions,' they'd say. They'd never believe us. If
we tell, it would make it all less than it is."

I heard Mom's voice as if she were in the
room: "Keep what's happened like a secret
in your heart, and it will be there always for
you." I knew then that we would do what-
ever it took to help the fairies.

CHAPTER ELEVEN

Jack and I were in my room, talking about the fairies.

"Did you feel it when you picked them up?" I asked.

"Yeah, it was really cool, The energy that comes from them when you touch them...I've never felt anything like it. Sort of like a slight electric shock, but it doesn't hurt."

"It makes you, like...glow. We've got to help them," I whispered. I looked over at the Victorian mansion and saw the gleam of a tiny lamp. I thought I had turned all the lights off.

"Can we keep them?" Jack's question distracted me, and it also upset me.

"Of course not! How would *you* like to be kept? They're as free as we are. We need to help them, not keep them."

"Okay. Okay, Nina. I'm going to go to sleep."

"Jack…," I began. "Oh, never mind. Fine. It's been a big day. Good night." I turned my light from dim to off, and fell asleep within minutes.

I don't know how long I slept, but when I awoke I noticed that all the lights were on in the Victorian. I looked at my window and saw it was still dark outside. Then I heard Jack jump out of bed, and it sounded like he was looking for something. I got up too, and went to see what was happening.

Jack was dressed and had his flashlight. Lily was flying around his head, flitting from one ear to the other. When she saw me she flew over and sprinkled my ears with fairy dust, and I heard her frantic plea for help.

"Hurry, Jack! Hurry, Nina! You must help us! We need you!"

I had no idea what was wrong, but I ran back to my room and threw on my jeans as Jack told me that Lily had flown out of the dollhouse just minutes before to tell him that Luna was dying. By this time Lily was sobbing, flying back and forth between the two of us.

"Let's go! Nina, let's go!"

Still not sure exactly what was going on and what we were expected to do, I quickly tied my sneakers while Jack explained the problem.

"We've got to carry Luna out of here as fast as possible," he said. Keeping the flashlight covered with his hand so that only a sliver of light escaped to illuminate our path, he led the way downstairs.

We went into the bathroom and looked for something to carry Luna in. I decided on Nanny's ruffled pink talcum powder box with the fancy powder puff in it. I thought of dumping the powder in the toilet, but I was afraid that if I flushed it down, the sound from the old pipes would carry through the thin walls and wake Nanny. She might come down to see if one of us was sick, especially since we had gone to bed so early. Instead I quickly emptied the powder into the waste-basket and covered it with toilet paper so she wouldn't see it and ask for any explanations. I made a mental note to empty the trash at the earliest opportunity. With all that was happening, I hoped I would remember.

I brought the box out, expecting to find Jack acting as lookout, but he wasn't there.

Through the window I saw him heading down to the screened-in porch facing the lake, where Dee slept on weekends. I followed him quietly, being careful to ease the screen door closed so that the spring wouldn't bang it shut.

"Dee. Dee. Dee!" Jack shook her awake.

"Huh, wha...what's going on?" She sat up and rubbed her eyes. "What time is it?"

"The fairies need our help, Dee," he explained.

"It's the middle of the night. Are you guys crazy?" she asked, now wide awake and a little angry.

"The fairies need our help, come upstairs!" he repeated, urgency in his voice this time.

"If you guys think...," she started.

"Please. Just come upstairs," I pleaded. "You're not going to believe this."

"Okay, okay." She slipped her jeans on over her long nightshirt.

"Shhh. We've got to be really quiet," Jack said as we neared the house. We snuck upstairs, not making any noise and stepping over the third step that always creaked, so as not to take the slightest chance of waking Nanny or Papa, who were sleeping in their room at the end of the hall.

When we got upstairs, I whispered to Dee, "Look in the Victorian mansion."

"You brought me up here to—," Dee started to complain loudly.

"Shhhhhhh!" Jack and I said together. "Just look!" We pointed to the tiny bedroom window.

Dee bent over and her mouth and eyes opened the widest I've ever seen anyone's open. "What? I can't believe my eyes!" She looked at us in amazement, and then looked back through the dollhouse window. "I can't believe my eyes," she repeated.

"Shhh!" we reminded her again.

"They're fairies Dee," I whispered. "Just like my mom told us about."

Dee got on her knees and nearly stuck her nose into the mansion. Finally she asked, "Are they real? Jack, let me see your magnifying glass!"

"No time for that!" he replied. "They need help. Let's see what Lily wants us to do."

"Who?" Dee asked, not taking her eyes off the fairies.

"Lily!" Jack answered.

I grew impatient with Dee and wondered if maybe we had made a mistake in waking her. But I realized that once she'd had a minute or two to adjust to the idea, she would be a big help.

"Lily is the girl fairy," I explained patiently, "and Luna is her brother. He's dying and they really need our help."

"Okay, okay," Dee answered, finally getting a grip on herself. "What do they need?"

"What do you need us to do, Lily?" I asked, inching closer to the mansion. She started to tell us but Dee interrupted.

"I can't hear anything," she said.

"Oh, I'm sorry," Lily said. "I forgot." She laid Luna's head on the miniature pillow and flew up toward Dee. Dee was startled but kept still. Lily sprinkled the magic dust on Dee's ears.

"Oh my gosh!" Dee exclaimed.

"Shhhhh," we again had to remind her.

"I can hear...well, everything!" she announced, sounding as excited as we had been when we'd first discovered our enhanced hearing.

"Fairy dust," Jack explained. "Now listen."

Lily began again, calmly but urgently. "If Luna is to live, we must bring him to the Crystal Cavern to restore his energy. For it is from the Crystal Cavern that all the energy comes. If he returns to bathe in the fresh springs of the lake waters, he will live. But if he does not get there in time, he will die! In the shadows of the cavern, to the east of the spinning wheel's needle, is the entrance to the tunnel, which will take us down to the depths of Dream Lake. The magic of the water will wash over him and he will regain his fairy magic and be well."

Lily asked Jack for paper. He ripped a piece from his sketchpad and she flew over it, tracing a map with the dust from her wings, like a printer using a stamp. When she was done we looked together at the map.

"Why, it's up Eagle Mountain, by the top!" said Dee.

"We need to leave. Right now! There's no time to lose." Lily flew circles around each of us, waiting for our response.

I slowly, carefully, and oh so gently laid Luna in the powder box. We headed downstairs, skipping the third step, and silently made our way to the front door. I used two hands to carry Luna's box. Lily flew just over my shoulder, keeping an eye on the box in case I stumbled. What she could have done if I dropped it, I don't know. But she was a fairy with magic powers, so I never doubted her. Anyway, there was no way I was going to let him slip. As we headed out, careful with the front door, the full moon lit the way.

"Keep the flashlight off," I whispered to Jack, knowing he'd use it at the soonest opportunity. We cautiously walked down the dirt road that led away from our house toward the path up Eagle Mountain. As we reached the base of the mountain, we heard barking that seemed to be getting closer.

"Sounds like a pack of wild dogs," said Dee. "I'll draw them away. Nina, you take Luna and start up the path. I'll cut through the woods and meet you up top."

"I'll go with you, Dee," Jack said.

"I had better go also," Lily said. "Dogs can be nasty."

"Okay," I whispered nervously, wanting to have someone come with me but too proud to ask. I didn't want anyone calling me a sissy. So, holding onto the box, I quickly started off into the darkness and up the path. Lily, Dee, and Jack went off in the direction of the barking dogs.

CHAPTER TWELVE

I followed the sound of the stream up the mountain path. I could feel the night eyes watching me from the surrounding woods. Nervously, I checked the powder box to make sure the fairy still lay in the padded bed of cotton balls. An eerie mist rolled in from the lake and climbed the mountain with me, dimming the moonlight and making the way treacherous.

I had to walk carefully to stay on the path and avoid roots, rocks, and other forest debris that could send me, and Luna with me, sprawling. While a fall might result in a skinned knee for me, it would certainly be much more serious for him. I might even lose him if I slipped.

"Stop worrying," I ordered myself. "Just pay attention. Be careful, but be quick. There's no time to waste."

As I walked, I went over Dee's directions in my head. "At the top of the mountain, when we reach the rocks, we'll need to look out for the old surveyor's markings, the ones your mom showed us. Then we'll need to pace off two thousand fairy feet to find where we are going."

The night's clouds parted and drifted off into the distant mountains as the evening cleared. I stood still for a moment getting my bearings and listening for sounds from the others. The fog on the mountain lifted as quickly as it had set in. I took a deep breath of the cool, moist air and began to feel calmer. I felt the moon pass overhead before

I saw it. Overbearing and full, it surrounded me with color and light so that I could easily find my way. We could do this!

In the distance, I heard the barking fade away. I looked down at the box in my hand, and at Luna, curled like a ball the size of a furry caterpillar. He was dying. With a renewed sense of urgency, I knew we didn't have much time.

"Jack! Dee!" I called. No answer. "Jack, Dee!" Again, no answer. I looked at Luna and knew I'd have to continue by myself. I moved more quickly up the mountain path. Crackling twigs somewhere in front of me caused me to stop and hold my breath. I squinted, looking for the danger that lurked ahead. A red fox trotted quickly across the path right in front of me. "Whew," I sighed.

I continued up, hearing more noises of the night as I went. I also heard more snapping twigs coming from the side of the mountain. Something larger than a fox was making that noise—a bear, maybe. I shivered. Then I heard my name in the distance. It was Dee.

"I'm here!" I called out, relieved.

"Where?" the voice called back.

"Here, over here!" I continued to call out until I could see Jack and Dee, arm in arm, walking toward me. Dee was hopping on one foot.

"I twisted my stupid ankle on a rock as we were running," she said. "It's killing me."

"How's Luna?" asked Jack.

"Worse. We've got to really hurry." I started up again, then stopped. Something was missing. "Lily—where is she?"

"We lost her when we ran from the dogs," Jack explained. "She drew them away from us. Last we saw, the dogs were chasing a little light that kept flying right at them before swerving just out of reach of their teeth."

"Well, we've got enough to worry about. I'm sure she can take care of herself," I said, to reassure myself as much as Jack and Dee. "Let's go!"

We moved on through the night, upward along the switchbacks of the mountain path. Dee found a walking stick and didn't need to lean on Jack anymore. She had a slight limp but walked quickly anyway. We barely had to slow our pace for her. But from time to time when I looked back at her, I caught a grimace on her face. "I'm fine," she said more than once, seeing my concern.

We eventually reached a clearing near the top of the mountain. I looked below and saw the moonlight glittering on the waves of the lake in the distance. *It must be near here*, I thought.

"Jack, get the flashlight," I said. "Look for the rock."

"It's much farther up the second viewpoint, don't you remember?" He had gotten ahead of us and was looking back over his shoulder, his flashlight pointed directly at me. Blinded temporarily by the beam of light, I didn't see a hole on the path and tripped. I felt myself falling and the box slipping out of my hands. I caught the small fairy in my hand as he flipped out of the powder box. Jack flashed the light on me again as Dee steadied herself.

"Come on! Get up, Nina, we're almost there," he called back to me. Excited about reaching the rock, he was apparently oblivious to how close we had come to a catastrophe. Taking the flashlight with him, he ran up the path, leaving me and Dee to stumble on roots and rocks. The woods were thick again, filtering out the moonlight and leaving the path dark.

"It's here! It's here!" he called down to us. "Grab the map, Dee!"

She pulled the wrinkled map from her jeans pocket. Fairy dust spilled out as she smoothed the paper. We all looked at it and searched for the mark of the surveyor's rock. I knew we had seen the rock by day, but the night woods played tricks on our eyes and we couldn't find it. Just then, a dart of light the size of a firefly flew between us and landed on my shoulder.

"Lily!" we shouted.

Sputtering and pointing, she tried to catch her breath.

"Had to take the dogs all the way down to the lighthouse...thought I'd never make it back. Luna, oh, Luna! There isn't much time!" She peered at her brother, lying still in the palm of my hand. "Follow me!" she ordered. She flew off and sparkled above the surveyor's rock.

Jack, having calculated that two thousand fairy steps equaled twenty of his own, began to pace off to the east. But when he stopped, there was nothing unusual, just a large rock formation.

"What now?" we cried.

CHAPTER THIRTEEN

A huge horned owl veered through the trees and came swooping over our heads. We ducked, and the owl soared up again before circling back and drifting down to land on a craggy boulder, ripped from the mountain and carried here by glaciers thousands of years ago.

"My friend is showing you the way. If he had sensed impure intentions, he would have driven you from the cave," Lily explained.

Just under the owl's perch, we noticed an opening in the boulder where the rock had split in two. One half of the rock must have been pushed by a glacier, while the other half was pulled. Smooth surfaces that mirrored each other were spread apart to form an opening just wide enough for us to slide through. At Lily's direction, we went in. Dee almost got stuck, but after a brief panic, she finally wriggled through.

With Jack's flashlight, we saw that the split rock led into a cavern so huge, Nan's house could easily have fit in it. Drops of water fell continuously from the ceiling, forming enormous stalagmite pillars that cast bizarre shadows in the flashlight beam.

Pink and purple crystals that cold marble grew up from the ground and down from the ceiling of the cave. Occasionally they connected to form crystal columns that reminded me of pictures I had seen of Greek temples. Although we couldn't see it, we could hear the sound of running water. Not a steady sound like water from a sink, but the swishing and gurgling sound made by a fast-running, mountain-fed brook after a spring thaw. The air was chilly with mist.

As we moved in farther, we were drawn to a brilliant white porcelain sculpture that grew right up to the roof of the cave. We were awestruck. Forgetting just for the moment our urgent mission, we approached the sculpture. Jack pulled out his magnifying glass and examined it more closely.

"Unbelievable," he said, almost to himself. Turning to us, he announced, "It's made of teeth!"

"Of course." Lily spoke from over my shoulder. "Where do you think the tooth fairies keep all those teeth?" Then she revealed the secret.

"The lost teeth of children are polished into the smoothest of stones. They are a treasure for us and are far more valuable than gold or diamonds are for humans. The teeth carry an aura of the pure spirit of children, not yet corrupted by adult reasoning and logic. The magic of the teeth of innocent children generates an energy that helps sustain the magical power of the Crystal Cavern. It began long ago with the pure spirit of a young Native American maiden.

"But enough of that," Lily said, shaking her head. "We must follow the brook."

I don't know how we hadn't noticed before, but the stream of water passed around the back of the sculpture and along the cave wall. Guided by Lily's sparkle, we followed the brook farther into the cavern. We went into more "rooms" like the one we had first seen, each as beautiful as the last, and each with its own sculpture caressed by the brook.

Winding our way in and down, deeper and deeper into the earth, we eventually came to a room that seemed endless. The beam of the flashlight was barely able to reach the high ceiling—over a hundred feet tall, at least. The far walls likewise were almost beyond the range of the light. And something else was different too. The bubbling of the brook hadn't followed us into this room. Instead, when Jack pointed the light down, we saw before us a smooth, shiny surface. At first I thought it was a giant mirror that reflected the pillars above it. But in a second, I knew it was a lake—Dream Lake, the magic lake we had come for.

"We're here!" announced Lily, her face tight with worry. She darted over to me as I laid Luna's motionless body down by the bank. Without a word, she took him in her arms and gently lowered him into the water. "Please," she prayed. "I hope we're here in time." She turned to us.

"You can help! Think positive thoughts, all of you! Please!"

We bowed our heads and thought of Luna getting well. I could hear Jack saying under his breath, "Come on, you can do it."

I pictured Luna flying, laughing, and dancing with his sister. I listened to the stillness of the place: the brook barely audible in the background, the occasional tinkle of the drops that fell from above into the lake and echoed in the cavern. It was so peaceful here. For the first time all night, I caught my breath. I *knew* Luna was going to be okay!

I opened my eyes and looked over at the fairies. Lily was slowly moving Luna back and forth in the water. I could see his skin returning to translucent white. Lily had a grin on her face that spread from tiny ear to tiny ear.

"It's working!" Lily cried. "He's going to be all right!"

Luna opened his eyes. "I'm okay," he said, winking at Lily. "Thanks to our friends here." He stepped out of the water and shook himself dry. He still looked tired, but seemed to gain strength by the second.

"Thank you. Thank all of you! How can I ever thank you enough for all you've done?" He looked at each of us in turn.

"Aw, it was nothing," Jack said.

"We will never forget you!" Lily insisted. She flew over to Jack and kissed his nose. He giggled and brushed her away.

Dee sat by the edge of the water and dangled her swollen foot into the lake. "Oh, this feels good," she said.

CHAPTER FOURTEEN

Dee slowly got up. She looked surprised as she gently pressed her weight down on her foot. "My ankle—it's all better!" she laughed.

A deep, calm voice seemed to come from the walls and echoed in the room with the lake.

"The magical energy of Dream Lake can do wonderful things, my dear," said the voice.

From across the lake, rays of light like shooting stars suddenly enveloped us. You would think we'd have been scared, but after all the strange new things we'd experienced in the last two days, talking walls of flashing light seemed pretty harmless. Besides, the voice sounded so calm, and, well, nice.

"Why, it's only Ray of Light from the Eternal Flame of Our Ancestors, Guardian of the Cavern," Lily volunteered. "We just call him Ray. I'm sure he won't mind if you do as well. He's very nice," she assured us.

As Ray zipped in front of us and stopped, I could see he was a beautiful fairy. His wings were the same color as the rose and purple tones inside the cave. His face was a pure, bright white without a trace of any other color. He had high cheekbones, a thin nose, and piercing brown eyes. His facial features, sharp and angled, resembled those of Native Americans. I don't know why, but I pictured him with a feather tilting down from the back of his head and reaching to his shoulder. I suddenly remembered the Native

American legends my mother had told us, and wondered if Ray somehow connected the fairies to the legends.

"Children," he said slowly, "thank you so very much for helping us." He smiled. "We can never thank you enough, for you have saved two members of our precious family. We know you are pure of spirit and free of selfish intentions, but no human has ever been here at Crystal Cavern. It is too dangerous for us. A slip of the tongue and we could be discovered by those who would capture us, put us on display, and eventually kill us. I thank you again, from all of us, but must ask you to please go now and never try to find your way back here. The entrance you arrived at will be sealed once again. The boulder will be rejoined, leaving no trace that it ever opened. Please follow me."

"Come. We'll go with you," Lily said, beaming. She turned to Luna. "Are you ready to fly?"

"Sure thing!" He did somersaults, twists, and turns in the air before us.

Ray beckoned us with his hand. Sparkling lights shot from his fingers as we followed him. He led us through a dark tunnel, his glowing figure lighting the way. "Up the ladder," he said as we arrived at a very short vertical stairway carved in the rock. Luna and Lily held hands, their wings fluttering contentedly.

I looked over at Jack, standing sheepishly by the fairies, and thought about how much I loved him.

Lily and Luna flew over and kissed us each on the cheek. "Thank you, thank you," the fairies said, waving goodbye. "We will never forget all you have done for us."

CHAPTER FIFTEEN

We climbed the ladder and came out on the mountain onto a bed of moss. I turned back toward the sound of voices and realized that the passageway through which we had just traveled was gone. It had vanished as if it had never been there. There was no mark in the moss revealing where we had come from. I dug down below the moss, into the ground, and found nothing but dirt and rocks.

"Most weird," said Dee. "I guess they don't want us coming back to visit." She grinned. We were all a little punchy from the adventure, excitement, and lack of sleep.

I suppose that's why we all lay on the ground laughing at Dee's joke until we cried. A few minutes later, we decided we had better get home, back to the safety of the reality we had known only the day before.

The full moon was directly overhead, lighting the woods as if a giant nightlight had been turned on. After the darkness of the caverns our eyes adjusted quickly, making it easy for us to find our way along a path that led down the mountain. I had never seen this path before, but it appeared that the fairies had made sure we would exit the cavern onto an easy trail. It was clear of rocks, fallen trees, overgrown bushes, and all the other obstacles common to any path in the woods. As we descended, the bats, hunting their nightly prey, swooped low and made fluttering shadows in front of the moonlight.

"Incoming!" yelled Jack, as he always did when bats flew near. We all laughed. It had been a marvelous night, one that made laughing easy. But it was late.

"I wonder what time it is?" he said, sounding tired. The adrenaline from our adventure seemed to be losing its kick. His eyes were droopy and I knew he must be exhausted.

"It's probably close to daybreak," Dee said. "If we hurry, we should be home and in bed before anyone knows we left."

The path curved to the left and abruptly ended at a moss-coated wall of rock. We sat down and slid over the rock. It was smooth and slippery-soft, like velvet. We slid on our butts so we wouldn't fall. "WooHOO!" we yelled in unison, tired but invincible.

Damp and slippery, we gathered speed and plunged down the side of the hill. When would the slide end? I grew more concerned as we picked up speed. The moss padded the rocks and cushioned our bottoms, so there was no problem until…SPLASH!

I was in the water. SPLASH! SPLASH! So were Jack and Dee. We had rocketed into an icy river and were quickly carried downstream by the swift current. Bumping against rocks, trying to hold onto something, grabbing, clutching, and then being ripped away, we were propelled into the rushing water again. The water finally slowed at a deep pool. I looked around and saw Jack and Dee bobbing along only a few feet from me.

"Everyone okay?" I called out over the river's noise.

"Yeah," answered Jack.

"I'm fine," yelled Dee. "Let's swim for the bank!"

But the current kept tugging us. "What's that noise?" Jack cried.

"Do you hear that, Dee?" I shouted.

The current grew stronger, forcing us closer to the sound. It was the sound of the river moving through the rocks that littered its bed. But it sounded stronger, more violent than the rapids we had already survived.

"Oh no! It's a waterfall!" Jack cried, and then the roar of the water drowned out his screams. Before we realized what was happening, we were being sucked under and through the flume, falling in a cascade of rushing water. We heard each other's screams as we plunged over the edge. Time slowed. It felt like a dream, a really bad dream.

I managed to cry, "Hang on, Jack!" as I lost sight of my little brother in the frigid mountain water. The cold took my breath away. Fortunately, the fall was short. But it was still terrifying.

Each rock we hit gave us another surge of momentum. At the bottom, another pool of water eased our tumble. I took the opportunity to look for my brother and my cousin. Jack came bobbing up behind me, and Dee was ahead. A dead tree had fallen over part of the river. As Dee passed it, I saw her reach up toward a broken branch. She held on as Jack and I floated toward her. She called to us to grab on. I latched onto the tree and snagged Jack as he reached out to me. We all gasped for air, unable to speak.

Finally Dee asked, "Are you guys all right?"

"I think so," I said.

"I hurt all over," moaned Jack. He looked as if he'd gotten the worst of the fall.

We pulled our dripping selves out of the river. "I think I'm okay," Jack said, wringing out his soggy shirt. "It just woke me up, that's all."

I rubbed his hair affectionately. "Okay, then. I've had enough excitement to last me a while. Let's go home. Carefully!" We were too tired to laugh this time.

"The sun's not up yet," Dee pointed out. "We can still make it before anyone sees we're gone."

We made it back home without further trouble, but we were totally exhausted. We snuck up the stairs, careful to avoid the third step, and slipped silently into our rooms. With all that had happened, I thought I would be too excited to sleep. But I was out as soon as my head hit the pillow, and morning arrived all too soon.

CHAPTER SIXTEEN

The next day, after a late breakfast, Dee, Jack, and I huddled together on the dock, talking about the night before.

"I guess Luna is going to be okay," said Jack, a tinge of sadness in his voice. It seemed like the end of a great adventure and we all felt a bit let down that it was over.

"I'm sure the fairies will go on with their lives as if we never existed," said Dee.

"Do you think we could find our way back to the Crystal Cavern to visit them?" Jack asked.

"Not a chance," I said. "Didn't you see how everything just disappeared as we left?"

We spent the day hanging out on the raft, working on our tans and diving into the water to cool down when we felt like it. Uncle Dennis, Dee's dad, took us waterskiing in the afternoon. Jack got up on his skis easily, but I still couldn't get the hang of it. Dee said I'd be up for sure by the end of the summer.

When we got back to the house and put the skis and life jackets away, we ran up to the house to see Mom and Dad. Nanny told us they had called to say they were running late but would be up for dinner. Jack and I looked at each other, disappointed that they would be late again, but happy that they would finally be with us soon. Nanny said they were probably going to skip a couple of days of work to stay with us, since the strange weather had altered their weekend plans.

We went to change out of our bathing suits. Dee's mom, my aunt Sara, looked out to where Dee's three-year-old sister Melanie had been playing in the yard by the old swing set.

"Kids!" she called. "Come get a snack. Dinner will be a little late tonight." We came running up from the lake toward the house. "Nina, Jack, is Melanie with you?"

"No, Aunt Sara. We've been fishing off the dock," answered Jack.

"Dee, she's not with you?" she asked, concern mounting in her voice.

"I thought she was at the side of the house with Scout," Dee answered, also sounding worried.

Aunt Sara rushed down to the lake and we followed, calling "Melanie, Melanie!" I ran out to the Point as fast as I could, looking on both sides of the beach for my little cousin.

"Melanie!" I heard them calling for her from the dock and from the woods.

"MELANIE!" we shouted, but no answer came.

CHAPTER SEVENTEEN

After our family and a few neighbors had searched for almost an hour, Aunt Sara called the nearby ranger station. She was frantic and unable to make sense. Papa got on the phone and explained the frightening situation. The ranger said that a search party would be put together and they'd be there to help soon. Nanny's face was ashen. "I hope she had the sense to stay away from the lake," I heard her say softly to Papa.

It was almost dinnertime, and of course nightfall wouldn't be far behind. Jack, Dee, and I went across the road and into the woods by our house again. Dee sat down on a rock and began to cry.

"What if we don't find her before night-time? She's all alone, Nina!"

Jack put his arm over her shoulder. "We'll find her," he said. "We have to."

"It's been over two hours now. What if she fell in the lake? What if she's lost in the woods?" Dee was now sobbing uncontrollably.

"Well, you don't have to worry about the lake," a soft voice said. "We've already made sure she didn't fall in." Luna and Lily were flying around us, sprinkling their dust on our ears and treading air before us.

"You're back!" I cried.

"Of course we're back. Well, actually, we never went anywhere. We're often around; people just don't usually see us. We heard the adults in your family talking," said Luna. "When we realized Melanie was missing, we immediately scoured the lake. The good news is that she is safe from the water. Unfortunately, that means she is probably in the woods. And the woods can be very dangerous for a little girl, especially after dark. You were so good to help us when we needed it. We are more than happy to help you now."

"Can you fly around to try to find Melanie?" asked Jack.

"We can do better than that," said Lily. "We can help you fly over the woods and look for her too!"

CHAPTER EIGHTEEN

It wasn't until much later that I heard the ranger's story. Dan Johnson had been sitting at his desk at the ranger station, checking the weather report from the top of Mount Washington. His radio chirped on and he listened to the news about the missing little girl down by the lake. He quickly checked his map to locate where she was last seen and saw that it was not too far from the station.

Ranger Johnson knew that the woods around the lake were no place for a little girl. Darkness was approaching and a search at night would be next to impossible. Gravel flew and dust from the dirt road followed his jeep as he sped to the missing girl's home.

He arrived at the house within twenty minutes. He spoke with the adults, assuring them that the Marine Patrol was searching the lakeside, and the police and our neighbors were looking along the roadways. The chief had advised him that a helicopter would be dispatched from Concord at dawn, should Melanie not have turned up by then.

Ranger Johnson told Aunt Sara he was sure the chopper wouldn't be necessary, that Melanie would probably turn up at a friend's house. But he said he'd take a look on Eagle Mountain, "just in case."

"Most of the large animals have headed for the deep woods, what with the summer folk being up and all, so she's really not in any real danger if she is on the mountain," he assured everyone. After getting a picture of Melanie from Nanny, he set off, driving up the mountain service road in his jeep.

The men with the dogs arrived at the house, and Uncle Dennis briefed them about where everyone was looking. Nanny retrieved one of Melanie's shirts from the laundry hamper and gave it to the man who handled the dogs, so that the dogs could sniff it and pick up her scent. Scout barked and whimpered as if she wanted to help with the search too. Nanny took her into one of the bedrooms and closed the door. Her muffled yelps grated on everyone's already-frazzled nerves until Papa went in the room, scolded her, and sent her into the corner, tail between her legs. Our family felt as anxious and helpless as Scout must have.

CHAPTER NINETEEN

The three of us looked at Lily like she was crazy. I knew the fairies possessed magical powers, but us, fly?

"Help us to fly?" I asked incredulously. "How can you possibly do that?"

In that calm and patient voice we had heard when she wasn't frantic over Luna's illness, Lily explained. "If you're willing, we can turn you into fairies for a short time. With a little practice, you'll be able to fly as well as we can."

"Will it hurt?" asked Jack, trying to sound brave. By nature, he liked exploration and change, as long as it didn't involve him personally.

"Of course not!" said Lily, losing a bit of the calmness in her voice. "After all you've done, can you possibly think we'd do anything that would hurt you?" Her voice was sweet again.

Dee said she didn't care whether it would hurt or not. Despite ditching Melanie sometimes, and getting mad when Aunt Sara insisted that the little one be allowed to tag along with us big kids, she really loved her sister.

"I'll do anything!" said Dee. "The sooner the better. Let's get going!"

"Sure. I'll do it if it'll help find Melanie," I added. I loved Melanie too, but that didn't mean I wasn't scared about this whole idea. On the one hand, it would probably be really neat, but…what if we couldn't get changed back? I mean, this whole fairy thing was really cool—Lily and Luna, Ray, Dream

Lake—but I didn't think I'd like to live in a cavern. I'd miss Mom, Dad, Nanny and Papa...well, I'd miss everything! No bedroom with the moose on the wall, no tuck-ins, no Sunday morning cartoons while Mom and Dad drank coffee and read the paper.

Interrupting my thoughts, Jack announced, "I'll do it too!" He stuck his chest out and stood up straight, like he was in a war movie and had volunteered to take on one of those missions where the sergeant says, "Only a few of you may come back."

Lily smiled patiently. As if reading our thoughts, she reassured us again. "It will only be temporary. We have done this before, so you really have nothing to worry about. It is very simple to do, and even simpler to undo. But of course, you must be sure that you want it to happen, or it won't. Now think about why you want to do it. If you have a selfish reason, it won't work, either. The only reason you want to change to fairies is to help find Melanie, right?"

We all nodded.

"Okay, then. I want you all to keep your thoughts and reasons pure. You want to find Melanie?"

We nodded again, and each answered in turn.

"Yep."

"Sure."

"Okay."

"Then let's begin." Lily nodded to Luna and they both gestured toward the sky. Their graceful arms reached up, index fingers pointed to the heavens, and they moved their arms in circular motions. Their right arms went clockwise and their left went counter-clockwise. Faster and faster they moved until they looked like rotors on a helicopter.

Suddenly the wind kicked up and whistled through the trees, almost like it was playing a song. The fairies were chanting something I couldn't understand. They were actually singing a strange gibberish—a fairy language, I suppose—in high-pitched voices. So high, in fact, that at times it hurt my ears, and at other times I think it was too high for us even to hear. I figured they were still singing because their mouths were moving just like they did when I could hear them. Maybe their highest pitches could be heard by dogs, like a dog whistle, because I could hear a chorus of howling in the distance. Their voices rose higher and louder, calling out to the trees, soaring upward toward the clouds.

In a flash, three small funnel clouds appeared through the trees and moved toward us. I suppose I should have been scared, but it was all so unreal, so magical, that I wasn't afraid at all. I looked at Jack and Dee. I could see they weren't scared either, just amazed. They stood perfectly still with their mouths open, forming little cartoonish "O's" of surprise.

The miniature tornadoes approached us, not in a straight line, but continuously toward us. It was as if they were dancing. They touched each other, joined together, whirled around one another, but always came closer no matter how they moved. Just before they reached us, maybe twenty feet or so away, they separated and stopped for a second.

The fairies continued to sing, higher and higher. Each of the whirlwinds then came directly, in an unwavering straight line, at each of us kids. I was completely calm, completely at ease, as one tornado washed over me. I could see Jack and Dee each being swallowed up into separate tornados.

If what has happened so far seems strange, what happened next is way too weird to even describe, but I'll try.

I was spinning as fast as the twister, but I wasn't the least bit dizzy. I could still see all around me as if I were standing still, but I knew I must have been spinning a thousand miles an hour. Around me, butterflies and brightly colored wildflowers spun, seeming to become part of me. I felt as light as a feather, but as swift and powerful as an Arabian stallion. Then a flash like lightning surrounded me, sending a painless but powerful surge of energy through my body.

The tornado stopped spinning, split open, and disappeared. Everything was calm, like the lake after a late afternoon summer storm, but even calmer, quieter. Everything seemed new, more colorful, brighter, larger. I looked at my hands, my arms, my wings...MY WINGS!

"Oh my gosh! *I'm a fairy!*" I yelled.

CHAPTER TWENTY

I looked over at Jack and Dee to make sure they were safe. I couldn't help but laugh when I saw them. This was thrilling! They looked at me and then at each other, and we all laughed. I guess you could say our laughter initially was brought on a bit by nervousness, but mostly, and then completely, by sheer joy.

"Look at you, Nina!" Jack exclaimed. "You're beautiful!"

"Well, look at yourself!" I couldn't stop giggling.

Dee instinctively began fluffing up and drying out her wings, like a butterfly emerging from its chrysalis. The damp glossiness disappeared as the wings dried quickly. But that's not to say that they weren't shiny—they still were, just not as glossy. In an instant, Dee jumped up and began flying.

Wings fluttering, stopping, beating rapidly, Dee flew all around us. She flew high and flew low as if she had always known how. Never one to be far behind, Jack took off, and after fluttering for only a few seconds, he began diving as if he were one of those fighter planes you see at an air show.

"Look at me!" squealed Dee. She'd been pretty to start with, but now, with violet wings, a silver body, and her long blond hair flowing freely around her, she was spectacular. Bursts of sparkling light shot out of her fingers into the air. I looked down at my hands and saw that I was doing it too. Unbelievable! It was like mini-fireworks flowing from my fingertips. I took off, soared, swooped, and dove; it was easy. Fantastic!

After another minute or two of flying, it seemed as if the three of us simultaneously remembered why we had become fairies. Within seconds, we fluttered smoothly down to earth next to Lily and Luna. We stopped giggling, stopped smiling, and looked at one another with serious expressions.

"Melanie," I said softly. "We need to start looking now."

"It will be dark soon," said Dee. "Let's go!"

Lily and Luna, who had been watching us with amusement, grew serious as well. Luna spoke. "We will spread out in groups. We can cover more ground if we split up completely, but you are new at this, and although I've seen your bravery, it would be foolish not to pair up. It is a beautiful world out there, but very dangerous when you are little.

"Nina and Jack, you team up and fly west. Lily, take Dee and fly east. My strength has fully returned and, as Lily will attest, I'm one of the fastest fairies around the lake. I'll be faster and cover more ground on my own. I'll go north, and if I don't find anything, I'll swing back and fly south."

Luna sounded like a general giving orders. He was very sure of himself, a far cry from the weak, limp fairy I had carried in Nanny's powder box. No one questioned him. We all just nodded.

"All right, let's head out!" Luna ordered.

"One second," Lily interrupted just before he took off. "Children, as Luna told you, it's a dangerous world for us, being so small. Most of all, you must beware of the bandits. They would like nothing more than to eat you for dinner."

With those words of warning barely out of Lily's mouth, Luna sprung up and away, followed in a split second by Lily and Dee, who headed east.

CHAPTER
TWENTY-ONE

Jack and I headed west, flying high above the trees. We flew like eagles. All of our senses were magnified. Our eyesight was so acute that we could clearly see tiny objects on the ground below us. Flying was such an awesome sensation—the wind in my hair, the cool breeze on the back of my neck, and floating in, or more like riding along, the wind currents. I felt as one with nature; I was light as a leaf fluttering through the sky.

But even with our superior eyesight, we couldn't see through the trees. Searching clearings, meadows, and roadways was easy, but we had to go down below the treetops to check the woods.

"Let's get closer," I said. He followed as we both swooped down into the woodlands.

"Beware the bandits," he joked. No matter the circumstances, he always seemed to have that sense of humor.

After flying between and around trees and not finding any clues to Melanie's whereabouts, we decided to land. Even though flying had seemed effortless high up, swooping in and out of the woods and avoiding trunks and limbs was tiring. We decided to take a little break from flying, just a minute or two. We landed side by side on a shiny green plant. Jack looked down at our tiny bare feet.

"Nina, is this poison ivy?" he cried.

"Oh no! I mean yes. If it has three leaves it's poison ivy!"

We hopped off quickly and landed on the mossy forest floor. From the ground everything looked so big.

"Geez," said Jack, "I hope these fairy feet protect us from poison ivy."

I looked over Jack's shoulder and froze. There was a huge, masked monster approaching from behind him. I couldn't get a sound out.

"A...a...a...BANDIT!" I finally managed to yell. It dawned on me what Luna and Lily had been warning us about when I saw the giant raccoon ready to pounce on Jack.

Seeing the look of terror on my face, Jack whirled around to see where my shaky finger was pointing. He looked straight into the black furry mask and snarling teeth of the enormous raccoon.

"Ahh!" he shrieked, falling back against a tree as the fiendish raccoon took a swipe at him with its razor-sharp claw.

"Nina! Help!"

Here we were, trying to be good, trying to find Melanie, and Jack was about to be killed by a murderous raccoon. This couldn't be! If you've ever heard those stories about how your entire life flashes before your eyes just before you're about to be killed in an accident, let me tell you that they are true. Except this time, it was as if I saw *Jack's* life flash before my eyes.

I saw him at the hospital as a newborn when I first got to visit him. I clearly pictured him as a baby, goo-gooing as I played with him. Then I saw him as a toddler, with a milk mustache and smashed peas on his cheek. I saw him in his Cub Scout uniform, carrying a tent and knapsack out to camp in the woods. And I saw him helping me make fairy houses—the houses we built playfully, wanting to believe they would be used but knowing we were really just pretending. And now here we were, really fairies ourselves, and Jack, because of our games, was about to die!

Trying not to panic, I glanced around for some way to escape, some way to save Jack. No way out! It just couldn't be real! But then miraculously, with the exceptional vision I had acquired as a fairy, I spied, directly behind Jack and cleverly camouflaged by pine needles and leaves, a chipmunk's hole.

"FALL BACKWARDS!" I yelled, rushing toward Jack faster than I had ever moved in my life. The giant slashing claw came down again. I grabbed Jack's leg and yanked him into the chipmunk hole. We tumbled down, arms and legs tangled, our bodies banging into the rocks, dirt, and debris that lined the walls of the chipmunk's tunnel. We landed in a heap at a spot where the tunnel leveled off and ran parallel to the ground, about twelve to sixteen "regular" inches down, I guessed.

I could still feel the frothy heat of the panting beast's breath. We were pelted by dirt and rocks that fell on us as the raccoon ripped at the earth, hoping to still salvage the meal that had unexpectedly escaped him.

"Deeper, Jack!" I cried. "He can still get us!"

I didn't have to say it twice. The tunnel was winding and dark, but it was wide enough for us to stretch out our wings and fly. We flew down slowly, carefully, because rocks that would have been pebbles in our "ordinary" lives were like boulders in our current state. We didn't want to start an avalanche that might close off our escape from the cruel bandit that still growled, at the entrance to the tunnel, for his supper. As we flew deeper and deeper into the tunnel, lit by the tiny beams of light shooting from our wings, we felt safer and safer.

"I...I think...I think we're safe now," Jack panted. "That raccoon can't dig this deep." He just stood there for a minute or so, looking down, hands on his knees, waiting to catch his breath. As his breathing slowed, he looked up at me in the twinkling light.

"Nina, you saved my life," he whispered, his eyes tearing up. "I sure love you."

"Aw, what are sisters for?" I shrugged him off, but naturally was very proud of myself. "You would have done the same. Now let's rest for a minute before we try to find another way out. Go on, sit down."

We sat down on round little seats for a minute or two, trying to compose ourselves.

I guess I must have gotten over the raccoon incident already, because my curiosity was kicking back in. Round little seats? I reached over to pick up another seat that was next to me, but couldn't budge it.

"They aren't rocks, and they couldn't be carved wood, could they?" I mumbled to myself.

Meanwhile, Jack wriggled around in order to get more comfortable on the round seat. The seat began to roll out from under him. "What the heck?" he gasped.

"Why, they're giant acorns!" I said. "Well, regular acorns, I guess,"

"Nuts!" he said as the acorn began to tumble out from under him. His "seat" rolled into another acorn, and that one into another, and in seconds they all began to roll.

"Nut avalanche! Hang on, Nina!" The acorns rolled down the tunnel, gathering speed and taking us down with them. Faster and faster we rolled, head over heels, smashing once again into the sides of the tunnel, but this time being clobbered by bouncing acorns, too.

After we find Melanie, I thought, *I'm getting changed back so I can lead a normal life.* I promised myself I'd never be turned into a fairy again.

Finally we hit another level area of the tunnel and stopped bouncing, landing on top of a pile of acorns. A final acorn bounced down and off Jack's head. What I heard him say at that moment I won't repeat.

"Are you okay, Jack?" I asked.

"I think so." He gathered himself up. "This place is almost worse than facing that raccoon. How are we going to get out of here?"

Beyond the nuts, I saw a pair of giant eyes looking at us.

"Now what!" I cried.

Jack saw it too. The creature was huge—compared to us, at least.

"Why, it's just a chipmunk," Jack said. "This must be his home we've been bumbling through. Don't worry, Nina. Chipmunks are herbivores. They eat nuts, berries, and plants, not people. Or fairies."

The buck-toothed chipmunk, his brown fur striped and velvety smooth, looked at us and his messed-up pile of nuts. He began chattering and I could tell he was furious. He was angry at us for messing up his house. You get this kind of sixth sense as a fairy, where you can understand what animals are saying better than humans can.

"We are so sorry," I said. "It was an accident. We didn't mean to intrude into your home, but a nasty raccoon tried to eat us." The chipmunk stopped scolding and nodded sympathetically. "Then when we sat down to rest for a minute, we accidentally turned your acorns into an avalanche. We really would like to get out of your hair—er, fur. Will you please help us find our way out of here? We won't bother you again."

Here I was, talking to a chipmunk! Even weirder, though, was that he seemed to understand everything I said.

The chipmunk nodded, chattered, and gestured for us to climb up on his fluffy tail. I shrugged at Jack. "Why not?" I said. We climbed onto his tail and held on tightly as our new friend scrambled up through the secret passages of the tunnel. He soon brought us out to daylight, in an area far from where we had fallen in.

"Thank you," we called, jumping off his back. He scurried away, stopping at the entrance to his tunnel. He looked back, chattered cheerfully, twitched his tail, and dove back into the hole.

"Geez, I guess we need to be more careful," Jack said. "This fairy business isn't as easy as I thought."

I was going to remark on the understatement of his conclusions but held my tongue. We dusted off the tunnel dirt and looked around, trying to get our bearings. We had lost our direction.

"Let's fly up and see if we can find the others or figure out where we are," I said.

"Okay," said Jack. And we were off again.

CHAPTER

TWENTY-TWO

I knew that Dee and Lily had headed east, around the mountain, and that we should be meeting up with them soon. Sure enough, Jack spotted them flying low, in and out of caves. We called out to them just as Dee emerged from a cave, looking frightened and upset.

"I didn't know we had bears on this mountain," she said.

"They keep to themselves, very deep in the woods to stay away from the summer people," explained Lily.

"I hope Melanie isn't near any bears," replied Dee with a shiver.

"We'll find her, Dee. I know we will," I reassured her, but she shook her head.

"Lily and I looked everywhere, and you and Jack didn't find her on the other side of the mountain. Now what do we do?"

"We'll fly even lower, nearer to the ground. There are four of us and we can cover more territory," I told her. "Melanie probably didn't go too far, but maybe she's hiding in a hard-to-find area, beneath the trees or behind some rocks."

We flew past a beaver building its dam and saw a spotted rabbit nibbling twigs in a woodsy meadow.

Lily turned her head so that one ear was toward the ground. "I think I hear something." "She's crying!" shouted Dee. "It's Melanie, and she's crying!"

Dee and Lily flew in the direction of the sobs, and we were right behind them. Curled up next to a large rock, crying inconsolably and hugging herself, lay Melanie. Dee and Lily swooped down to within inches of her face. Melanie sat up when she saw their fire-fly sparkles.

"It's okay, Melanie, I'm here," Dee reassured her. Melanie's eyes grew wide and she just stared at her sister's fairy face. "It's okay, Melanie, it's me!"

Jack and I both told Melanie how glad we were to see her, but she didn't respond. Just then, Luna appeared and joined us as we stood in front of Melanie.

Poor Melanie didn't know what to look at first. Her sister and her cousins were fairies. She looked from one of us to the next in shock, not understanding, but not crying anymore either.

"It's okay now, Melanie," Dee kept saying. She tried to hug her but couldn't get her tiny arms around her giant little sister.

We heard the sound of an engine approaching in the distance, its four-wheel drive shifting gears as it climbed the rugged terrain.

"There's not much time," said Luna. "Someone's coming. Hurry!"

Luna and Lily raised their hands toward the sky and began singing their magical song once again. Just like before, the wind blew hard through the trees, pine needles scattered across the ground, and the tornadoes appeared. Melanie screamed as they came toward us. As quickly as before, the tornadoes washed over us. Spinning and twirling, we were all caught up in our own storm once again. The only difference was that the tornadoes seemed to be going in the opposite direction, and the flower petals and other bits of nature's treasures seemed to be thrown out of the tornadoes, not sucked into them.

I soon found myself falling onto the ground, landing next to Dee and Jack, who were sprawled out, changed back to their normal selves again. I was back to me, too! Melanie rushed into Dee's arms as a forest ranger pulled up in his jeep. The fairies vanished.

"You found her! Good work, kids. Is she okay?" He looked at Melanie, who was sobbing again.

"She's okay now, sir," Jack replied confidently. "She'll be fine."

"How did you kids get up here before I did? I've got a jeep. How were you able to find her on this vast mountain?" asked the ranger.

"Oh, we're always exploring up here, sir," Jack said. "We know this mountain inside and out." He winked at Dee and me slyly. We giggled at his joke.

Jack and I hopped into the jeep, and the ranger helped Dee lift Melanie up and secured them both in one seat belt. He slowly drove us down the mountain and back to Nanny and Papa's house. The ranger radioed ahead, so Aunt Sara, Uncle Dennis, Nanny, Papa, and our parents, who had arrived while we were gone, were all in the driveway to greet us.

Melanie was swept up into the arms of her parents. Jack and I yelled, "Mom! Dad!" and ran into their arms as if they'd been gone for a thousand years. So much had happened; our lives had changed forever since we had last seen them.

"Looks like she's none the worse for it. She'll be fine," the ranger told Papa, who had stepped forward to shake his hand. There was backslapping by the men and crying by our moms as we headed into the house. Neighbors who had helped with the search filled the house. Nanny and Mom put out food and drinks as more and more people came by.

Dee, Jack, and I just hung out looking at all that was going on. Melanie was home, and we had rescued her.

CHAPTER
TWENTY-THREE

A few days later things returned to normal. Dee and her family left for the city
on Monday afternoon. Mom and Dad left us
late Monday night, but they said that the

next week we would all spend a long week-end together at the lake. Jack went back to trying to win a place in the *Guinness Book of World Records* for the most sunfish caught off the dock. Now I had time to sit up on my cliff, to think and to write.

We never told Mom about the fairies, but I could tell by the way she looked at us after we'd rescued Melanie that she knew. I've seen the little shell ships on the beach and other signs of the fairies since then. Jack and I were talking and he thinks that if we build the houses again, the fairies might come back. I'm not so sure. But I am sure that I'll always remember that summer, and the secrets we learned at the Crystal Cavern.